NO FIGHTING,
NO BITING!

by ELSE HOLMELUND MINARIK

pictures by Maurice Sendak

Author and artist of LITTLE BEAR

NO FIGHTING, NO BITING !

An I Can Read Book®

HarperCollins*Publishers*

CONTENTS

COUSIN JOAN

"Cousin Joan,

I want to sit with you,"

said Rosa.

"I want to sit with you, too,"

said Willy.

"Sh-sh-sh," said Cousin Joan,

"I want to read."

"Willy, you are squeezing me,"
said Rosa.

"I was here first."

"You are squeezing me, too,"
said Willy.

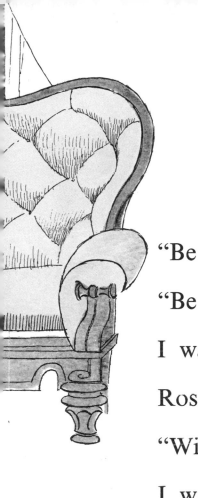

"Be still," said Cousin Joan.

"Be still.

I want to read."

Rosa whispered,

"Willy, you are squeezing me.

I was here first."

Willy whispered,

"You are squeezing me,

and you are squeezing Joan,

and I was here, too."

9

Joan said, "I just cannot read
with you two squeezing.
"Willy, you sit here,
and, Rosa, you sit here.
Now be still.
I want to read."

Rosa whispered again,

"Willy, you did squeeze me,

so I will pinch you."

And she pinched.

"Ow! Who pinched me?"

said Cousin Joan.

"Oh, Joan!" said Rosa.

"I wanted to pinch Willy, not you."

"And she squeezes, too," said Willy.

"Do you know what you two are?"

said Cousin Joan.

"You are little alligators.

Now be still.

I want to read."

Rosa whispered, "Joan — —"

"Sh-sh-sh!" said Cousin Joan.

"But, Joan," said Rosa.

"Now what?" asked Cousin Joan.

"Why are we little alligators?"

asked Rosa.

12

"You are not really little alligators,"
said Cousin Joan.

"But you do things like little alligators."

"How?" asked Willy.

"You squeeze and you pinch,
and I cannot read," said Cousin Joan.

"See, here is an alligator.

Here is an alligator in my book."

· ✦✦✦✦ THE ALLIGATOR ✦✦✦✦ ·

Willy said, "But he is a big alligator,
and he looks hungry."
"Yes," said Cousin Joan,
"and when he is hungry,
even little alligator children are not safe."

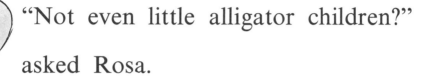

"Not even little alligator children?"

asked Rosa.

"Not even little alligator children,"

said Cousin Joan.

"Now, I want to read."

"Cousin Joan," said Willy,

"tell us a story.

Tell us about a big, hungry alligator."

"Yes," said Rosa.

"And about alligator children."

"No!" said Cousin Joan.

"I want to read now."

"But, Joan," said Willy,

"you always tell such a nice story."

"Yes, Joan, you do," said Rosa.

"Do I really?" said Joan.

"Oh, yes!" said Rosa and Willy.

"Well," said Joan,

"if you really think so,

and you really want a story,

then maybe I can tell you one."

"About alligators!" they said.

"Yes, about alligators," said Joan.
"About two little alligators
called Light-foot and Quick-foot."

17

LIGHT-FOOT and QUICK-FOOT

Once there were two little alligators
called Light-foot and Quick-foot.
One morning, Mrs. Alligator said,
"Come along now, children,
we are going fishing.

18

"I want you to hurry,
because I am very hungry."
"Good," said Light-foot,
"I'm hungry, too,"
and he bit Quick-foot's tail.

"Ow," said Quick-foot,

and he bit Light-foot's tail.

"Come, come, children, no fighting,"

said Mrs. Alligator.

"No fighting, and no biting.

Come along now, and hurry!

HURRY!"

They all went along the alligator path.

Soon they came to a big log.

Mrs. Alligator climbed over the log,

and she did it very nicely, too.

But Light-foot and Quick-foot

did not do so well.

Light-foot climbed up a little way,

but then he fell down on top of Quick-foot.

So Quick-foot bit him.

Then Quick-foot climbed up a little way,

but he fell down on top of Light-foot.

So Light-foot bit him.

Then, of course,

they were fighting again.

Now! Who should be coming along

but a big, hungry alligator.

And when big alligators are hungry,

even little alligator children are not safe.

Light-foot and Quick-foot saw him,

and they stopped fighting.

"Well!" said the big, hungry alligator.

"Well, well!

Two nice little fat alligators.

Too fat to climb over the log."

"We are not too fat!"

said Light-foot and Quick-foot.

"The log is too big."

"So, the log is too big, is it?"

said the big, hungry alligator.

"I will help you over the log."

"How?" asked Light-foot and Quick-foot.

"Well," said the big, hungry alligator,

"I can't put you on my back,

because if I do, you will fall off.

"But if I open my mouth," he said,
"you two can get in.
Then we can all go over the log."

He opened his mouth wide,

and Light-foot and Quick-foot looked in.

"You go first," said Light-foot.

"No, you go first," said Quick-foot,

and he pushed Light-foot.

Just then Mrs. Alligator called.

'Children, if you can't hurry,

I'll give you you-know-what."

That made Light-foot and Quick-foot hurry.

They forgot all about the big alligator.

They climbed over the log quickly,

all by themselves.

And they hurried along till they came

to Mrs. Alligator.

Now all three went along very nicely,

Mrs. Alligator, Light-foot and Quick-foot

They went along the alligator path

till they came near the water.

Then Light-foot and Quick-foot

saw some eggs.

"Look at the eggs!" they said.

" We want to eat them!"

"Very well, but hurry," said Mrs. Alligator.
"I will go down along the path,
and I will be in the water, fishing."
Light-foot said, "I count three eggs.
I will eat two."

Quick-foot said, "I count three eggs.

I will eat two."

"Two are too many for you,"

said Light-foot.

He bit Quick-foot's tail.

"No! Two are too many for you,"

said Quick-foot,

and he bit Light-foot's tail.

Then, of course,

they were fighting again.

Now!

Who should be coming along the path

but the big, hungry alligator.

Light-foot and Quick-foot saw him,

and they stopped fighting.

"Well," said the big, hungry alligator.

"Well, well.

My two nice little friends.

What are you doing here?"

"Counting eggs,"

said Light-foot and Quick-foot.

"Counting!" said the big, hungry alligator.

"You can't count."

"Oh, yes, we can,

we can so count,"

said Light-foot and Quick-foot.

"If you can count,"

said the big, hungry alligator,

"maybe you will count my teeth.

I have always wanted someone

to count my teeth.

I will open my mouth wide.

Then you two can get in

and count all my teeth.

All the way to the back of my mouth."

So the big, hungry alligator

opened his mouth wide,

as wide as he could.

Light-foot and Quick-foot looked in.

"Wow!" said Light-foot.

"Look at all the teeth!"

"And look at all the teeth in the back!"
said Quick-foot.

"Go in and count them," said Light-foot.

"No!" said Quick-foot.

"You go in and count them."

"No! I'm going fishing," said Light-foot,
and off he went.

"I'm going, too," said Quick-foot,
and off he went.

"STOP!"

roared the big, hungry alligator.

But Light-foot and Quick-foot

were on the way down to the water.

In the water they went.

Splash! Splash!

And right after them came
the big, hungry alligator,
and in the water he went.
SPLASH!

NOW!

What should he bump into

but Mrs. Alligator.

"How do you do?" she said.

"Looking for something?"

"Ub!"

said the big, hungry alligator.

"Ub," he said again.

"Oh?" said Mrs. Alligator.

"I think I have to go now,"

he said.

"I should think so," she said,

"or I may have to bite you."

"Good day, Ma'am," he said.

And he hurried away

as fast as he could go.

Light-foot said, "He ran after us."

Quick-foot said,

"He was not very nice, was he?"

"He is hungry," said Mrs. Alligator,

"and you look just like fish to him."

"Do we?" they said.

"Yes," she said.

"Another time, don't stop to fight,
and don't stop to talk.
Do you hear me, you two?"

"Yes," said Light-foot and Quick-foot.

"All right," she said, "now fish."
So they fished.
And it was good that they did,
because they were really very hungry.

'That's all," said Joan.

'Now I can read."

'But I want to know something," said Willy.

'Where did the big alligator go?"

'Oh," said Joan. "That's another story."

ON THE WAY HOME

"Tell us," said Rosa and Willy.

"Very well," said Joan. "Here it is."

The big alligator went fishing,

but not near Mrs. Alligator.

He had all the fish he wanted,

and that made him very happy.

Then he went back along

the alligator path.

Soon he came to the big log.

What should he see there

but Light-foot and Quick-foot.

They were on the way home,

and wanted to climb over the log.

They could not do it,

because they had eaten too many fish.

The big alligator said,

"Well, well.

Can't climb over this time, can you?

I will help you."

"We can't talk to you,"

said Light-foot and Quick-foot.

"We have to run now."

"Ho, ho," laughed the big alligator.

"Don't run.

I will push the log away."

So he pushed the log away.

"Bye, now," he said, "be good,"

and off he went.

Just then,

Mrs. Alligator came along.

Light-foot said,

"The big alligator pushed the log away."

"Did he!" said Mrs. Alligator.

"Yes," said Quick-foot,

"and he said for us to be good.

Are we good?"

"Yes, of course," said Mrs. Alligator.

"Are we always good?" asked Light-foot.

"Well, you are good little alligators," said Mrs. Alligator.

"But when I say no fighting,

NO FIGHTING!

And when I say no biting,

NO BITING!

And when I say come along, COME!

Do you hear, you two?"

"Yes," said Light-foot and Quick-foot.

"Good!" said Mrs. Alligator.

"Now come along."

So they all went along the path.

"And that's the end of the story,"
said Joan.

ROSA'S TOOTH

"Ooh," said Rosa.

"What is it?" asked Joan.

"My tooth!" said Rosa.

"When you talked about alligator teeth,
I wriggled my tooth, and it came out.

"Now I have lost it."

"Well, let's look for it," said Joan.

Rosa and Willy and Cousin Joan

looked for the tooth.

But the tooth could not be found.

Rosa began to cry.

"I wanted to put it under my pillow."

Willy said,

"Rosa says the fairies take her tooth,

and put something under her pillow."

"Yes, they do," said Rosa.

"They know that my tooth came out.

And if my tooth is not under my pillow,

they will think I have forgotten them."

Cousin Joan said,

"Maybe they will know you have lost it.

Anyhow, they will always know

that you have not forgotten them."

How can they tell?" asked Rosa.

They can tell just by looking at you,"

said Cousin Joan.

Can they really?" said Rosa.

But if there is no tooth,

will they put something under my pillow?"

I think they will," said Joan.

They may put something under your pillow

that is just right for you."

"What could that be?" asked Rosa.

"It could be a little ring," said Joan.

"It could be a little ring
with a blue forget-me-not on it.
Would you like a little ring
with a blue forget-me-not on it?"

"I would love it," said Rosa.

She had stopped crying,

and now she was nearly laughing.

Willy said,

"Here's the tooth.

I was sitting on it."

"Sitting on it!" said Cousin Joan.

"My! My!"

"Yes," said Willy, "now let's all read.

You can read, and we can read.

Rosa can sit with me."

'All right," said Rosa.

'And let's all be still," said Joan.

'Willy," said Rosa, "you are squeezing me."

'You are squeezing me, too," said Willy.

Cousin Joan said,

"I may have to do something

about you two.

Willy, are you squeezing Rosa?"

Willy said no.

"Rosa, are you squeezing Willy?"

she asked.

Rosa said no.

"Then no one is squeezing," said Joan.

No, no one was squeezing.

"Or fighting?" asked Joan.

Oh no, no one was fighting.

"Or biting, maybe?" she asked.

No, no, no.

No one was biting.

"Good," said Cousin Joan.

"That's just right.

Let's read."